# THE BOOTY



## DEVNEY PERRY

# OTHER TITLES

## Calamity Montana Series

The Bribe

The Bluff

The Brazen

The Bully

The Brawl

The Brood


## The Edens Series

Christmas in Quincy  Prequel

Indigo Ridge

Juniper Hill

Garnet Flats

Jasper Vale

Crimson River

Sable Peak


## Treasure State Wildcats Series

Coach

Blitz

Clifton Forge Series

Steel King

Riven Knight

Stone Princess

Noble Prince

Fallen Jester

Tin Queen


Jamison Valley Series

The Coppersmith Farmhouse

The Clover Chapel

The Lucky Heart

The Outpost

The Bitterroot Inn

The Candle Palace


Maysen Jar Series

The Birthday List

Letters to Molly

The Dandelion Diary

Lark Cove Series

Tattered

Timid

Tragic

Tinsel

Timeless


Runaway Series

Runaway Road

Wild Highway

Quarter Miles

Forsaken Trail

Dotted Lines


Holiday Brothers Series

The Naughty, The Nice and The Nanny

Three Bells, Two Bows and One Brother's Best Friend

A Partridge and a Pregnancy


Standalones

Ivy

Rifts and Refrains

A Little Too Wild

# AUTHOR'S NOTE

Once upon a time, a girl met a boy who won the Wrangler Butt Contest at the annual Testicle Festival in Bozeman, Montana.

The girl married that boy.

And they lived happily ever after.

(Also, the boy doesn't know that the girl is using said real-life experience as inspiration for this story. She can't wait to see his face when he finds out.)

CHAPTER ONE

"PUT THAT DOWN." I swatted at the red Solo cup in Joann's hand.

"Hey!" She dodged my attempt, clutching it tight. "Knock it off."

"Where did you get that?" I scanned the crowd. "Who poured it for you? Were you watching? What if someone dropped a date-rape drug in there?"

"Ugh." She rolled her eyes. "Stop being such a downer. I watched the dude pour this. And now I'm going to drink it."

"But it's . . . *beer*." I cringed as she chugged.

A dribble of white foam escaped the cup and her lips, falling down her chin and landing on the dirt beneath our shoes. She pulled the cup away, sighed and—"Burrrp."

"You are so attractive right now," I deadpanned.

"Then it's a good thing I'm not here to find a man."

"Why *are* we here?" I asked as a man bumped into my

shoulder, jostling me around. All night I'd been touched by strangers. Not even my masseuse was this handsy.

"It's fun, Lola." Joann smiled, her eyes slightly unfocused.

"Oh, you are drunk."

"That's the plan." She hiccupped. "Will you lighten up? Let's parrrr-ty. Whoop!"

"I'm going to have to hold your hair back later, aren't I?"

"Wouldn't be the first time." She laughed. The three tequila shots she'd slammed before we'd left her house were clearly numbing the pain.

That pain and my duty to support her through this life change were the only reasons I was here tonight, standing in a monstrous barn.

On Valentine's Day.

At the Testicle Festival in Calamity, Montana.

When she'd told me the name of this party, I'd laughed, certain she'd made it up. Nope.

"Should we go get a testicle?" Joann giggled, knowing it would make me cringe. Again.

"Please stop saying testicle. I beg you."

She stuck out her tongue. "Testicle. Testicle. Testicle."

I closed my eyes and visualized myself in a happier place. At home in my apartment, with a glass of wine, a good book and chocolate.

The waft of frying oil and beer batter snapped me back to reality—the Testicle Festival. Or Testy Fest, as Joann and the locals had so affectionally shortened it. Vinyl signs hung on the barn's steel walls. Banners streamed above the two portable bars, each set up at opposite ends of the building. The logo for the event was a cartoon bull, his rear end proudly displayed and his large testicles swinging free. They'd even branded a heart into the bull's side, in honor of this Hallmark holiday.

"Aren't they called Rocky Mountain oysters?" I asked.

"Technically. If you want to get fancy."

"I always want to get fancy." Tonight, there wasn't a lick of fancy to be found.

I'd been to Calamity a handful of times over the years. After Joann had married Riley, they'd moved here for his job with the forest service and to be close to his family, who lived around this area of Montana. And on occasion, I'd traveled here to visit my best friend.

In the summer, we'd go hiking in the mountains. In the winters, we'd drive to the closest ski hill and spend the day on the slopes and drinking hot cocoa in the lodge. Calamity had that small-town Montana charm. It was peaceful. Friendly.

The locals must have been on their best behavior during my previous visits because tonight their true colors were showing. There was nothing quiet about this party. It was raucous and rowdy. Raunchy and riotous. I'd been adding *r* adjectives to my list since we'd walked in the door.

Joann glanced around the crowd, her lips moving, but I couldn't make out a word she was speaking over the noise coming from the live band.

"What?" I shouted.

She leaned in to talk directly in my ear. "I said, let's get in line."

Before I could protest, she latched on to my wrist and dragged me through the crowd toward the line of patrons waiting to collect their oysters. We dodged drunken cowboys as we moved. There were young adults—kids—who didn't look old enough to be holding keg cups. Every other woman was dressed in a thin tank top and Daisy Dukes.

"It's fifteen degrees outside."

"What?" Joann said.

"Nothing." I waved her off. *What am I doing here?*

This was not how I'd planned to spend Valentine's Day. This was not how I'd planned to spend my trip to see Joann.

But from the moment I'd arrived in Montana earlier today, Joann had been acting off. She was too chipper for a woman about to get a divorce from the love of her life. I'd planned to spend time with her and learn more about the downfall of her marriage than I had on our phone calls over the past month. Except she hadn't stopped moving long enough for me to investigate.

First, we'd had to drop off my things. Then we'd had to get changed. And after those tequila shots of hers and the announcement we were headed to a party, I knew things were much, much worse than I'd imagined.

Joann was devastated and doing her best to hide it behind that pretty smile. No matter how many times she said how glad she was to be divorcing Riley before they had kids, I saw straight past the ruse.

This was heartache. This was desperation. This was drowning her misery in some cheap booze because she wasn't ready to face the fact that her marriage had imploded.

"Uh, Jo." I leaned in close as we finally reached the end of the line. "Is Riley going to be here tonight?"

She shrugged. "Probably."

"Is that why we're here?"

"No!" She said it too loudly and too quickly.

*Ahh.* Now the party made sense. We weren't here so she could get wasted and forget her sorrows. We were here to spy.

It was almost cute how she'd thought she could hide her motivations from me.

My friend was hoping to run into her soon-to-be ex—either to torture him or torture herself—and to see exactly what he was up to since she'd booted him out of their house one month ago.

"Jo, let's get out of here," I said. "If you want to get drunk, then we'll pick up some vodka on the way home. But if this is about Riley—"

"It's not about Riley."

"Oh, Joann. My sweet, sweet Joann. You've never been good at lying."

She raised her chin. "This is one of the biggest events in Calamity. It raises a lot of money for the food bank, and I want to show my support. Can you just loosen up for like an hour?"

"Nice try. I'm still not buying it."

"Gah. It's infuriating how well you know me." She huffed. "Fine. You're right. I want to see if he came here with *her*. One hour. Please?"

I groaned. "One."

Then I was dragging her out of here, driving her home

and taking a long, hot shower to wash away the stench of fried bovine testicles and sweaty humans.

Valentine's Day was supposed to be spent in pajamas with an aroma therapy candle. Instead, I'd been avoiding beer spills for the past hour. Cupid had sent me into the pits of hell this year. Apparently, hell smelled like Bud Light and grease.

"I'm too old for this kind of party," I muttered.

"Ha!" Joann chortled. "In college, you'd always say you were 'too busy' for this kind of party. Now you're 'too old.' You're twenty-eight. And look around."

There were people of all ages here. "Do me a favor? Don't do air quotes. You look ridiculous."

"Says the woman wearing a pair of ballet flats, a twin set and pearl earrings." She gestured to my wardrobe. "I told you to change."

"This is just like everything else I brought. Maybe if I had known that a barn dance was on the agenda for the week, I would have packed differently."

"You look like a lawyer." She reached for my cardigan, fumbling to unbutton the top button.

"Stop that." I swatted her away, redoing the button and righting my cardigan. "And I am a lawyer. Part of the reason I'm here this week, remember?"

"I remember." Sadness washed over her face and Joann lifted the beer cup to her mouth, chugging until it was empty.

"Jo—"

"I'm good!" She smiled.

No, she wasn't. But when she needed to cry later, I'd

be there. And if this party was her chance to confront Riley, then I'd stick it out too.

A man passed us, a red-and-white-checked paper boat in his hand holding a steaming fried hunk of meat. Was a testicle considered meat?

"Are you really going to eat one of those?" I saw food poisoning in her future.

"They're actually good."

I gagged. "Pass."

Joann giggled and looped her arm with mine, resting her head on my shoulder. "I'm glad you're here."

"Me too." I held her arm tighter.

She'd called me a month ago to tell me that she and Riley had separated. Until that call, I hadn't had the faintest clue that they were having problems. Certainly not the kind of problems that had led him into the company of another woman.

According to Riley, he hadn't cheated on Joann. I was inclined to believe it was true. Riley didn't seem to be that sort of man. And I think Joann believed him too, which was why she was calling it an emotional affair.

So I was here to act as moral support—and to make sure the lawyer she'd hired wasn't a complete pushover—as she and Riley negotiated the terms of their divorce.

A divorce she didn't want. Because although he'd hurt her, Joann was wildly in love with the man walking our way.

"Oh shit," I muttered.

"What?" She stood straight.

"Smile." I forced one of my own. "You're having the best time ever."

"What are you—" The words died on her tongue when she spotted him.

Joann had come here tonight to see Riley, but I suspected she'd underestimated how it would make her feel. Her entire body stiffened, but my girl wasn't going to admit defeat. She put on a beaming smile, swished a lock of her long, brown hair and laughed.

Riley flinched when he heard it, hesitating a step, but then he came over, his hands tucked into his jeans. Thankfully, he was alone, or his testicles might have been the next to land in the frying pan. "Hey, Jo."

"Hey," she said, feigning indifference.

"Didn't think you'd be here tonight."

"I come every year. Why would this year be any different?"

"I, uh . . . guess it's not." He rubbed the nape of his neck, then looked to me. "Hi, Lola. When did you get to town?"

"Earlier today."

He nodded, his gaze darting between me and his wife. "That's good."

The line shifted forward and Joann took a step, hauling me with her as she raised her chin and dismissed Riley.

He stood there, rooted as he stared at her profile. Agony was etched across his features and the urge to hug him was so overpowering that I almost caved, but then he disappeared into the crowd.

"Is he gone?" she whispered.

"Yeah."

"Phew." Her body sagged.

"Maybe we should skip the, er . . . *food?* And get you another beer."

"Maybe that's a good idea."

We left the line just as the live band ended their blaring, country rendition of "You Shook Me All Night Long."

"All right! All right! Who's ready for some fun?" the lead singer and emcee drawled into the microphone. His voice had a rough edge that lent itself to the country and rock covers he'd been performing all night.

Joann and I were swallowed up in the noise as the crowd screamed, our journey to the beer garden halted as all eyes focused on the stage.

"On behalf of the Calamity Food Bank, we want to thank you for coming out tonight. This has become a notorious fundraiser in the past three years, and because of your support, we'll be able to feed hundreds of people in need around the county."

Applause bounced off the walls. I'd never heard so many whistles and catcalls over a charity.

Okay, so maybe it was clever. The food bank was offering food that was definitely . . . unique. And with the twenty-five-dollar cover charge and the bodies packed into this place, they had to be bringing in some cash.

"Now this year's a special year. We got lucky and the event fell on Valentine's Day. So to all you lovers out there, let's see you give your Valentine a little kiss."

"Ugh." Joann and I groaned in unison as couples around us kissed and hugged.

The singer put his fingers to his lips and let out an ear-piercing whistle. "That's a lot of love. But in honor of

Valentine's Day, we've come up with a little something special for the single ladies in the room."

I swear, that man picked me out of the crowd and his gaze locked on me.

"I can't be the only single woman in the room," I muttered as the color flushed my cheeks.

The singer clapped his hands together, rubbing them as an evil grin spread across his face. "Folks, let me explain to you how this is going to work. This is what we're calling the Wrangler Butt Contest."

"The what?" I was the only one confused.

Everyone else started whooping and cheering. Even Joann had a genuine smile on her face.

The singer looked stage left and waved up a group of men, some more eager than others, to shuffle onto the stage. The man at the back of the line was practically being shoved up the stairs by his buddies.

"These fine gentlemen, many of whom you recognize and love, are gonna put on a little show for you single ladies. Rules are simple. Cheer for the guy with the best Wrangler butt."

If the noise earlier had been deafening, this was explosive. The walls rattled and the floor shook as the ten men took their place in a line across the front of the stage.

The singer picked up his guitar and backed away, giving the men space as the band began playing an upbeat rhythm. Was this really happening?

"This is—"

"Awesome!" Joann cheered with her arms raised in the air.

"Barbaric. I was going to say barbaric."

"Would you stop?" She clapped, her *let's have fun* mood back after the encounter with Riley. "When did you get so serious?"

"Law school."

She threw her arms around me, laughing as the music picked up tempo. "How can you not think this is hilarious?"

"It's mildly entertaining, in a meat-market sort of way." The first man started dancing, though dancing was a generous term. "Is that supposed to be twerking?"

Joann was laughing so hard she had to dab away tears. "That's Hal Miller. He's a fireman in town. His wife is right over there."

"The pregnant one?" I asked as my gaze followed her pointing finger to the woman holding her belly with one hand as the other was cupped to her mouth while she shouted. "So much for a show for the single ladies. Seems like false advertising."

Of the next eight men who twirled and shook their assets for the crowd, only one was single. Joann told me about each of them, how they belonged to her community and how she knew them from her time living in Calamity.

Then it came to the last man. The one who'd been shoved onstage by his friends.

The music played but he stood statue still in his spot at the end of the line. His thick legs were planted wide and his muscled arms were crossed over his broad chest. The definition in his biceps was visible even from across the room.

My mouth went dry as I drank him in. Dark hair, disheveled and slightly too long. A narrow waist. Flat stomach. Those Wranglers seemed tailor-made for his long, long legs. *Wow*.

"And who is that?" Why was it so hot in here?

"I don't know." Joann tapped her chin. "He looks familiar but I don't think I've met him before."

Whoever he was, he was not having any part of the festivities. The band played and he simply stared at the crowd, unmoving.

"Well, I guess we know who's coming in last place," the lead singer taunted.

The man shot the singer a glare and then his entire demeanor changed. He shoved past the other competitors and strode across the stage, stopping dead center. A smirk stretched across that delicious mouth, and with one swirl of his hips, he ensnared every female in the room. Even the married ones.

The energy in the barn skyrocketed. The man danced and every gaze was fixed on his perfect, firm, round ass. Never had I seen such a muscled behind. My palms itched to slide along its curve and squeeze it tight. Damn, but he could roll his hips. No doubt I wasn't the only woman in the room with damp panties. A dull ache bloomed in my core, a pulse of heat and desire I hadn't felt in a long, long time.

"You're drooling, Lo." Joann flicked my chin.

"No mortal man has an ass like that."

"Too bad this is barbaric."

"Totally barbaric," I muttered.

The music stopped too soon. The man shot the crowd a devastating grin and jerked up his chin to the other men on stage.

He knew. The entire barn knew.

*No contest.* He might not have wanted to perform, but that hadn't stopped him from dominating the entire competition.

"Come on." Joann took my elbow and nodded toward the bar in the corner. "Let's get a drink."

After the victor was announced, the band resumed their set while the contestants shuffled offstage. From the corner of my eye, I caught some back slaps and arm punches to the winner, but then I lost sight of the contestants as Joann pulled me through the masses.

"Jo, wait up." I nearly tripped on a man's boot, catching myself before I could fall and be trampled by the couples doing the jitterbug and two-step. But she was on a mission.

"Shots!" Joann's arms flew into the air when we reached the bar.

"You're so going to puke on me later."

She laughed and held up two fingers for the bartender. "Tequila."

"I hate tequila shots," I grumbled. "And I'm driving."

"Who said one was for you?" She downed the first shot, then the second, her face souring at the burn. I barely had time to slap a twenty on the bar before she bolted for the crowd again.

"I'm too old for this." I chased after her only to find her dancing with a cowboy who looked equally as inebriated as she was.

"Ouch." The woman from another dancing couple stepped on my toe. Then a man slammed into me. "I'm going to die out here."

I made a break for the edge of the room, pushing and

shoving my way past bodies, hoping for a moment of respite, when once again, the pointed toe of my Italian leather flats caught on a boot and I went sailing.

"Oof." My knees crashed into the dirt floor, but I managed to catch myself before face planting. My blond hair flew into my face, the curls that I'd done this morning before I'd caught my flight out of Portland now limp and hanging in my face. So it took me a moment to register that my hands were braced on something hard and hot.

And round.

And covered in denim.

*Oh. Sweet. Jesus.* My hands were on an ass. A very tight, very firm ass.

I pushed the curtain of my hair aside, and sure enough, there it was. The leather Wrangler patch stitched into the dark-wash pockets was right in front of my face.

"I'm sorry. Shit." I shoved up to my feet. "I'm so sorry."

My face was as red as the plastic cup in the man's hand. With a fortifying breath, I forced my gaze to his face, only to have the air sucked out of my lungs when I locked with a pair of dazzling hazel eyes.

"It's you. The Wrangler Butt guy."

The grin I'd seen on stage spread across his handsome face. Then he winked and my entire world turned upside down. "Aiden Archer."

# CHAPTER TWO

"LET'S GO, JOANN."

"I'm coming." She walked out of the kitchen, attempting to put on a shoe with one hand while holding a travel mug in the other and a piece of toast between her teeth. With the shoe on, she straightened and took hold of her breakfast before it could fall to the floor. "Ready."

"We're late." I opened the door and the cold blasted me in the face. "Gah."

"Oh shit." Joann looked outside, spun away from the blizzard swirling and raced through the house.

"Where are you going?" I called after her.

"I have to change shoes."

"But we're late!" I glanced at my watch for the tenth time in as many minutes. The mediation meeting with Riley and his lawyer was starting, well . . . now.

"I hate being late," I muttered to the empty room, tapping my foot on the floor.

Above me, Joann was rifling through her closet. The

muffled noise of shoes being tossed this way and that drifted through the ceiling.

Finally, Joann's footsteps came pounding down the stairs. She rushed into the living room, having lost her toast and coffee somewhere along the way. Instead of the heels she'd had on, there were knee-high riding boots over her black skinny pants.

Joann darted to the coat rack, pulling on her parka. Her gaze dropped to my own feet. Feet clad in heels much like the ones she'd deemed inappropriate for the snow. "Do you need to borrow some other shoes?"

"There's no time." My feet might freeze off, but the clock was ticking. "We're late."

I opened the door again and walked into the storm, trudging through snowbanks and drifts to her car parked in the driveway. The wind bit into my cheeks and snowflakes burrowed into my hair.

There wasn't much relief from the cold inside her car either. The frigid leather of the seat seeped into my thin black slacks, and even with my down coat, my goose bumps were growing goose bumps.

"Holy shit, it's cold." Joann started the car and reversed out of her driveway, punching buttons to get the seat warmers going.

"Maybe you shouldn't have put all of Riley's stuff in the garage on Saturday night."

"Maybe you shouldn't have ditched me to hook up with the new guy in town."

"I didn't ditch you." I'd been very responsible and driven her home. I'd made sure she was tucked into bed with a glass of water and two Tylenol on the nightstand.

Then I'd ditched her to hook up with the new guy in town.

Aiden had followed us to Joann's house. He'd waited in his truck while I'd helped Joann inside. Then he'd driven me to his home, where I'd spent the night—the best night—in his bed.

Meanwhile, while Aiden had been giving me orgasms, Joann had woken up and decided that having Riley's belongings in her closet was a problem she intended to remedy immediately. That was why she couldn't park in the garage and we were risking hypothermia on the drive across town.

Joann had heaped Riley's clothes into a pile. She'd thrown shoes and boots haphazardly into the mess followed by a video game console and a box of old photos. She'd even managed to drag his favorite recliner into the mix.

I should have been there to help her. Or stop her.

"I'm sorry, Jo. I don't know what I was thinking going home with him."

"I'm kidding." She looked over and smiled. "I'm glad you had some fun. I'm proud of you. That's a very non-Lola type of thing to do."

"I blame the testicles. And the Wranglers. And the fact that I haven't had a decent orgasm in years."

Besides the occasional blind date disaster, no man I'd met had piqued my interest over the past few years. Certainly not one I wanted to sleep with. My constant companion as of late had become work, and the men I'd met hadn't stood a chance at stealing my attention.

Until Aiden.

After a couple of dances at the party and a tempting kiss in the middle of the crowd, he'd most definitely had my attention. And when he'd asked me to spend the night with him, I'd been helpless to resist.

One night of passion and I felt lighter than I had in years.

"Are you sure you don't want to see him again?" Joann asked.

"Absolutely not."

Aiden had returned me to Joann's the next morning, and after a kiss on the cheek, we'd gone our separate ways. It was a onetime thing.

"You could hook up while you're here."

"No. It was just for a night. A change in my Valentine's Day routine of books, wine and pajamas. But it ends there."

"Why? You said the sex was good."

"Fantastic." I shivered, just thinking about the way that man had toyed with my body, bringing me to the edge time and time again before finally toppling me over.

"You're the only woman in the world who's scared of good sex."

I frowned. "I'm not scared. I'm just realistic. What happens if we hook up again and it's not fantastic? Sex that incredible never happens twice. I'd rather have the good memory, thank you very much."

"But what if it keeps getting better?"

"It won't." First-time sex was always the best. Maybe because my expectations were low, but whenever I'd had repeat lovers, the enjoyment had always dwindled. "Let's talk through this meeting."

Joann groaned. "Do we have to?"

"Yes."

Yesterday, I'd let her dodge my questions and change the subject whenever I brought up her impending divorce. But with the meeting happening in minutes, I wasn't walking into the mediation room without a little bit of preparedness. "What did your lawyer say?"

"Just that I should come to the meeting with a list of things I want."

"Anything else? What did he say during your preparation meetings? Did he explain the process for you after this initial meeting?"

"No. Sort of. Not really."

I bit my tongue. I wasn't a divorce lawyer, and I wasn't licensed to practice law in Montana. My role here was moral support and counsel because Joann didn't like her attorney. The options were limited in Calamity, and rather than postpone this divorce to find new representation, she'd bulldozed forward in true Joann style.

She was so desperate to divorce Riley and rid herself of this hurt that she wasn't thinking. Emotions were in control. Which was why when she'd asked if I'd come to Montana and sit in on this meeting, I'd cleared my calendar and booked a flight.

I suspected that her lawyer was lazy and saw this as an easy payday. But I wasn't lazy, and I wouldn't allow her to get steamrolled by whatever hotshot attorney Riley had drummed up.

"What's on your list?" I asked.

"My car. The house."

"Okay." Both were doable, especially since Riley had

moved into a cabin owned by his parents. Since he had a place to live, it made sense to let Joann keep the house they'd been renting while saving up to buy something of their own. The same was true with the vehicle. He had his own truck and didn't need her SUV. "Anything else?"

"Half the savings. I just want to split everything."

"Seems fair."

"And . . . Clarence."

*Shit*. "Joann. No. You can't be serious."

"I bought Clarence."

"As a gift for Riley." We both knew it would rip Riley to pieces to give up the golden retriever. And he'd fight to the death to avoid losing his dog. The old adage, a man's best friend, had never been truer than between Riley and Clarence.

Hell, Clarence was the reason they were getting divorced in the first place.

Irreconcilable differences? No. The reason cited should be *puppy*.

I was in Montana during a winter blizzard, preparing to sit beside my best friend as she faced off against her husband, all because Clarence had run away from home.

It had happened this fall. Clarence had jumped their yard fence, and a neighbor two blocks away found him and called Riley, even though Joann's number was listed on Clarence's tag. But that neighbor had set her sights on Riley, and Clarence gave her the means to attack.

The woman struck up a friendship with Riley, and because he was a man—i.e., clueless—he thought nothing of spending time with her as a friend. They took their pups on walks together. Those walks turned into weekend lunches at the local café.

Riley confided in her that Joann was struggling to get pregnant. The neighbor sent the gossip all over Calamity. Joann started to receive looks loaded with pity wherever she went. She had strangers approach her at the coffee shop and offer advice on the best sexual positions for conception. Even her boss at the hospital where she worked in Human Resources offered to set her up with a specialist.

Joann was humiliated. What she saw as her greatest failure—even though it wasn't a failure—was splashed all over Calamity.

Because Riley had befriended a jealous, devious bitch.

He apologized. He cut all ties to the woman. But the damage was done.

Not only did the rumors of Joann's infertility—or speculated infertility, because she had yet to see a doctor—spread like wildfire, rumors that Riley was stepping out on her also came to life.

Riley swore he hadn't cheated. That he'd never cheat. Maybe if he had spent more time with his wife and less time with his dog and neighbor, Joann wouldn't doubt him.

His betrayal broke her heart.

Her doubts broke his.

A month ago, they'd gotten into a huge fight and he'd walked out. The next day, she'd told him to get a lawyer.

Now, here we were.

At her lawyer's office.

Joann parked two spaces down from Riley's truck. She

gave the vehicle a sneer as we rushed inside to escape the cold.

"You're late," the receptionist greeted.

"The roads are so icy," Joann lied.

"Everyone is waiting." The receptionist waved us past her desk and into a conference room where the sound of male voices filled the air.

I picked up Riley's voice, gentle and kind.

But there was another. Why was that chuckle so familiar?

I followed Joann inside the room and my stomach plummeted. *Oh fuck.* A pair of brilliant hazel eyes stopped me cold.

"Aiden." My breathy whisper filled the room as each person looked my way. But my focus was on the man who'd danced across a stage Saturday night. The man who'd played my body like a concert violin. The man I hadn't expected to see again.

Aiden stared at me for a long moment but there was no surprise on his features. Before I could make sense of why his jaw wasn't flapping open like mine, he cleared his throat. "You're late. My client only has an hour for this meeting."

*My client.* Aiden was a lawyer.

And he was sitting on the wrong side of the table.

No. That son of a bitch.

He wasn't surprised to see me because he knew exactly who I was.

Before I could leap across the table and choke the life out of that lying, scheming bastard, Joann linked arms with mine and marched us to the table. Her gaze was locked on her husband.

Riley was wearing an olive-green shirt and he looked like, well . . . shit. Complete shit. Had he been drinking? His eyes were bloodshot. His face had a gray pallor. And his hands were jittery, tapping in quick succession on the table. *Tap. Tap. Tap. Tap.*

That was going to get old. Fast.

Aiden must have thought the same thing because he reached over and placed a palm over Riley's hands, then gave his client a reassuring nod.

"You're late." Joann's lawyer leaned in close as we sat down, repeating the obvious. Joann put me in the middle seat and I fought the urge to plug my nose as a waft of his coffee- and cigarette-infused breath hit my nostrils.

"Sorry," Joann said. "But we're here now, so let's just get this over with."

She cast one more glance at Riley, then dropped her gaze to the table. Waves of pain and heartache radiated off her body. They were coming from Riley's direction too.

I reached under the table, fumbling for her hand. The moment it was in my grasp, she gripped my fingers so tight my knuckles cracked.

"Shall we begin?" Aiden picked up his pen and reviewed the sheet in front of him. "Who wants to go first?"

"We will." Joann's lawyer sat straighter in his chair. "My client would like the house, her car and a dog. Er . . ." He fumbled with his own papers, searching for a sticky note. "Clarence."

Riley's eyes went wide as Aiden chuckled.

"Anything else?" Aiden asked.

"All other assets to be divided equally in half."

"Anything else?" Aiden asked again.

Joann's lawyer shook his head. "No."

The air in the room went silent and static. Aiden stared at Joann's lawyer, his gaze unwavering. Tension mounted as I held my breath, but I'd been in this situation many, many times before.

The first person to talk was the loser.

Joann's lawyer kept his mouth shut. Maybe he wasn't such a fool after all.

Riley looked like he was about to come out of his skin as the clock on the wall ticked. Joann's grip began to shake.

I felt it before the eruption. The crack that would give way to the flood.

One moment it was quiet. The next, everyone started talking at once.

"The dog is nonnegotiable. Clarence stays with Riley," Aiden said.

"You're not taking my dog, Joann. He's mine!" Riley shouted.

"He's my dog," Joann seethed. "I bought him."

"We can revisit the dog," her lawyer said, earning a glare.

"I hate you for doing this!" Riley shot out of his seat.

"Me?" Joann was on her feet next. "You made me do it! You were having an emotional affair. You told that woman our private business. How can I ever trust you again?"

"I didn't know. I was just walking the dog. My dog."

"And flapping your gums, telling our secrets, while you

walked *my* dog." She pointed to her chest. "I bought the dog!"

"And gave him to me." Riley planted his hands on the table and leaned forward. "You're not taking him. You're not taking everything away from me."

"What have I taken from you?" Joann tossed up her hands.

"How about my couch?"

"This is going well," I muttered as the two of them delved into old arguments.

Riley was a clean freak. Joann was too messy. She'd spilled marinara sauce on his couch and the stain had never come out, so she'd bought a new one online without consulting him first. The couch argument morphed into others. Riley forgot her mother's birthday. Joann never liked his grandfather.

As the couple raged, I dared a glance across the table at Aiden.

His eyes were waiting.

"You knew who I was," I said.

He gave a single nod. "I did."

"And you didn't think it was worth mentioning that you're Riley's lawyer? Say . . . before you took me to bed?"

"Not really."

My blood began to boil. He'd duped me. He'd tricked me. Later, I'd feel ashamed for not seeing him for the snake he obviously was. But for now, I was going to embrace my cold, icy rage and get some answers. "Did you think it would help with this mediation?"

"No."

"Then why?"

"I have a theory. You were out for a good time on Saturday," he said. "We had a good time."

That good time was now ruined thanks to the truth. The bastard. He'd tainted three—*or was it four?*—perfectly amazing orgasms.

"Why didn't Joann recognize you?" My friend was too busy screeching at her husband for me to ask her.

"I'm not from Calamity."

"Where are you from?"

"Prescott. A town about an hour from here."

I blinked. "Then where did you take me on Saturday?"

A grin tugged at his mouth. "Riley's place."

My jaw dropped. "What?"

"He was already passed out. You were too busy sucking on my face to notice."

Oh. My. God. I'd slept with the enemy under another enemy's roof. And to his point, I'd been so consumed with Aiden that I hadn't even noticed.

When Aiden had carried me inside, we'd been a tangle of limbs and lips. I'd had my legs wrapped around his Wrangler-clad ass and he'd had his hands under the waistband of my pants.

"Was this a trick? Was that why you took me to Riley's place?"

Aiden leaned his forearms on the table. "No trick."

"So you're just a liar."

"Lawyer. We pronounce it lawyer. What are you doing here anyway?"

"I'm a lawyer. Me. A good lawyer. You are a liar."

He shrugged. "Semantics."

How could I be so reckless? As a woman who prided

herself on rational thought and self-control, Aiden had been a momentary weakness.

But I'd liked him. I'd liked his honesty—or what I'd thought was honesty. There had been no question that he'd found me attractive and his no-nonsense invitation to his bed had been refreshing.

The crackle between us made it hard to breathe. Even now, it carried across the table.

Except it was all bullshit. It made no sense why he'd take me home. There was nothing to gain here. He hadn't even known I'd be at this meeting. Though Riley might have speculated that since I was in town, I'd tag along. Had Aiden taken me to bed simply to unravel Joann? To brag that he'd screwed her best friend?

Maybe he thought . . . it didn't matter.

"You used me."

"Just like you used me. Isn't that why you 'crashed' into me? Because Joann sent you my way to try and get information for this mediation?"

"What? You're delusional."

"Whatever you say, honey. You two played me how you wanted. Except I got to play too."

"I had no idea who you were. Neither did Joann."

"Maybe. Or maybe this is all an act. Doesn't matter. I got what I wanted."

Sex. He'd gotten sex.

My hands balled into fists. "I think I hate you."

"I hate you!" Joann screamed.

Riley's wince shook his whole body.

"I think we're done here." I shot out of my seat. "Come on, Joann."

She linked hands with mine as her lawyer sputtered for us to stop. We ignored him and marched for the door. My temper was so hot that I didn't need my coat when we walked outside and into the snow.

"He's Riley's lawyer." Joann let out a fuming growl. "Ahh!"

"I didn't know." I held up my hands. "I'm sorry. I didn't know."

"So he lied to you."

"Yup."

She jutted out her chin. "Then we'll make them both pay. Get in."

"Where are we going?" I asked, getting into her car and buckling my seat belt.

"Aiden must be one of Riley's friends from Prescott. They must have grown up together. Riley didn't talk about him, but you know Riley. He has a million *friends*."

She hissed the word *friends*, probably because she was thinking of his neighbor *friend*.

"Aiden took me there on Saturday," I said. "To Riley's. The lying jerk."

She gave me a maniacal grin. "Feel like getting even?"

"Yes." Revenge wasn't something I indulged in often, but for this, I'd make an exception.

Joann drove us to Riley's house, returning me to the scene of Saturday night's crime. She went to the kennel and proceeded to steal her dog.

Then she stood by watching as I raided Aiden's overnight bag. He must have planned a few days in Calamity, probably for the party and for this mediation. He'd packed some extra clothes. A razor. Deodorant.

And a toothbrush.

I scrubbed his toothbrush in Riley's—unfortunately clean—toilet.

Revenge wouldn't be sweet this time around. No, it would taste like toilet water.

*Take that, Wrangler ass man.*

# CHAPTER THREE

"YOU."

I glanced up from my laptop and frowned. "Me."

"Are you following me?" Aiden asked.

"That's my line, Archer."

"Eck." He recoiled. "You've degraded me to my last name."

"Goodbye." I fixed my attention back on my screen and poised my fingers over the keys, but Aiden's shadow didn't disappear. "You're still here."

"Is something wrong with your table, sir?" The waitress appeared at his side, two glasses of water in her hands.

"Table's great." He winked at her. "Thanks."

My stomach dropped as she set the waters at the table directly beside mine. *No.* I didn't even try to hide my groan.

What had I done to deserve this? I donated to charity. I was nice to children and dogs. I paid my taxes and voted in every election. So why was I being tortured by this infuriating, deceitful—albeit gorgeous—man?

Aiden stepped between our tables, shrugging off his coat, giving me a direct view of that perfect ass.

Damn him. That butt was the reason I was in this predicament. The reason why I couldn't enjoy a peaceful working lunch. With Aiden close enough that I could smell the spicy cedar tones of his cologne, there was no way I'd be able to concentrate on returning emails.

*Focus, Lola.* I shook my head and reread the email I'd been reviewing when Aiden had arrived. Then I clicked reply and began my response.

"What are you working on?" Aiden's breath caressed my cheek. There was cool mint on his breath, the same mint that I'd taken into my mouth. The man must love his gum.

I leaned away before memories of Saturday got the best of me. "Do you mind? This is confidential."

"Sure it is," he deadpanned.

"This town is too small," I muttered. In Portland, I didn't have to worry about running into a one-night stand. Not that I had many—any—one-night stands to run into. "Is there a reason you're here? Other than to torment me?"

"Lunch of course. How was your sandwich?" He gestured to the remnants of the BLT and a few forgotten fries on my plate.

"Please go away."

"You go away."

"I was here first." All that was missing from my declaration was a foot stomp and a harrumph. Then I would have nailed the line like a four-year-old.

That bastard had baited me.

Aiden smirked, then his gaze drifted across the room toward the door and his expression morphed. Gone was the evil twinkle in his eyes. A smile stretched on that chiseled face and my heart skipped.

*Oh, stop.* My physical reaction to him was getting old. But even after learning of his deception in yesterday's mediation meeting, I couldn't seem to ignore his presence.

His smile showed straight, white teeth. I'd licked those teeth. He'd used them to tear off my panties. His cheeks creased with lines around his mouth, most likely because he laughed and smiled often.

He'd probably laughed after duping me into his bed.

I hated him. *Remember, Lola?* Hate.

Following his gaze across the café, I spotted a woman coming our way. A beautiful woman. That stung. Just days after he'd lavished me with attention and orgasms, he was on a lunch date.

Wait. My stomach pitched. "Is that your girlfriend?" I hissed.

Aiden didn't answer.

I frantically searched her hands for a ring. Aiden didn't wear one, but she had a coat draped over her arm, hiding her left hand.

"Are you married?" Please, tell me I hadn't slept with a married man.

"Jealous?" Aiden asked, sliding from his seat as the woman approached.

"Answer the question."

Of course the jerk didn't answer. He just kept on smiling as the woman rushed into his open arms.

She gave him a tight hug and her own smile was nearly as blinding as his. Then she draped her coat over the back of a chair and her hands began moving, communicating to him using sign language.

Aiden laughed at something she signed, then he signed back, his lips moving with each word. He wasn't as fast as she was but certainly fluent.

They spoke and I stared unabashedly, lost in the grace of their movements.

I'd always thought sign language was beautiful. In college, there'd been a student in one of my political science classes who'd required an interpreter. I couldn't recall the professor's face for that course because during every lecture, I'd find myself staring at the interpreter's hands instead of the man speaking.

Aiden gestured to the table and pulled out the woman's chair, holding it for her as she took a seat. Then he bent and brushed a kiss on her cheek before returning to his own place, the chair directly beside mine.

This was a cute café but they needed to put more space between the tables.

The woman looked around and her eyes landed on me.

*Busted.* I'd been staring. My cheeks flushed and I zeroed in on my screen.

"Don't mind Lola," Aiden said, speaking to the woman, his hands moving in the corner of my eye. "She's wondering if you're my girlfriend or my wife since I slept with her on Saturday night after the Testicle Festival."

My jaw dropped as my face whipped up to his.

The woman giggled, covering her mouth with a hand. Her left hand. No ring.

I wasn't a homewrecker. *Oh, thank God.* But he'd made me out to be a slut.

My face felt ten times too hot. The last time I'd been this embarrassed, it had been during junior year of high school PE, when the teacher had made us play basketball. One of the boys had done a bounce pass my direction and instead of catching it with my hands, I'd caught it with my nose.

To this day, I didn't touch balls.

Except Aiden's.

My blush deepened. Seriously. Why couldn't I stop thinking about Saturday night? This was all his fault. The conniving, sneaky—albeit sexy—man.

"I hate you," I declared.

"You said that yesterday."

"And it's still as true today as it was then."

"This is my sister, Aspen," Aiden said, signing as he spoke every word. "Aspen, this is Lola Jennings."

I blinked, startled not only by his sister but that he'd remembered my last name. "H-hi."

"Hello," she said with a wave. "Nice to meet you."

"You too."

Aspen's hazel eyes were as bright as Aiden's. Her chocolate-brown hair hung in straight, silky locks. Unlike her brother, she owned a comb.

"She's beautiful." Aspen's voice had a unique tone, but it was sultry and her words clear.

"Thanks," I said as Aiden said, "Yes, she is."

I shot him a glare. He didn't get to compliment me. Not today. Not after embarrassing me in front of his sister and surprising me as Riley's attorney.

Aiden, immune to my scowl, simply chuckled. Did he actually enjoy it when I was angry? The sadistic snake.

"Do you live here?" Aspen asked, twisting in her seat to face me instead of her brother.

"No, I live in Portland."

Even as I spoke, Aiden signed. But it was clear that Aspen didn't need it.

"She reads lips," Aiden said. "And she has cochlear implants so she can hear. Obviously, she can speak. We sign out of habit, I guess. And because then we can talk about you and you won't know what we're saying."

Aspen signed something to him with a scowl.

"She called me an asshole."

I laughed. "She's not wrong."

That only made his smile widen.

The waitress returned and took their order. I used her as an excuse to refocus on work and attempt to repair the invisible boundary between my table and theirs. It was pointless. The moment the waitress left, Aiden came crashing in.

"Lola's in town helping a friend through a divorce," he told Aspen.

"I'm not talking to you about that. You're the enemy."

"You know what they say about enemies." He winked. "Keep 'em close."

That wink. Why was it so charming? I hated cheesy, winking men. But it wasn't cheesy with Aiden. It was . . . foreplay? Well, he could save those winks for some other unsuspecting woman. There'd be no more romps in Riley's guest bedroom for me.

I turned my attention to his sister. "Do you live in Calamity? Or are you just visiting too?"

"I live here." She nodded. "I work for the school district as an interpreter. Now that Aiden's back in Montana, I make him drive over to visit me at least once a month."

"You know you missed me," he teased.

She smiled at him and the love there was impossible to miss. As an only child, it was hard not to be jealous.

"If you weren't in Montana, where were you?" I asked Aiden. "Visiting Lucifer in the pits of hell to pick up some tricks?"

Aiden chuckled. "Close. I went to law school in Texas."

"What do you do, Lola?" Aspen asked.

"I'm also an attorney. I practice in Portland."

"But you're not licensed in Montana?" Aiden asked.

"You know I'm not. Otherwise we most definitely wouldn't be speaking."

Aiden leaned deeper into his chair, relaxing like he owned the place. His confidence oozed into the restaurant. It was what had drawn me to him on Saturday. I'd always been a sucker for a man who knew exactly what he wanted. And even though I'd die before admitting it, his confidence in yesterday's mediation was part of what had flustered me so thoroughly.

That and his lies.

I was normally the person in the room with the most confidence. I was the woman in charge and rarely did someone take me by surprise, especially when it came to legal matters. Yesterday, Aiden had turned the tables and I'd lost my composure.

He was doing the same thing now. Aiden watched me like he had me all figured out. He watched me like he was sitting on a secret.

But I'd learned my lesson yesterday and now my guard was up.

And not just with Aiden.

There was a twinkle in Aspen's eyes that made me nervous. She kept looking between me and Aiden, and I wasn't sure if she was relying on him to interpret for her, or if it was something else.

"What kind of law do you practice?" she asked.

"Let me guess." Aiden held up a hand before I could answer. "Personal injury?"

"You're infuriating," I murmured, then put on a smile for Aspen. "I work with kids. I'm a public interest attorney. Mostly, I specialize in work with children, doing foster care advocacy. Lately, my firm has taken on some cases to help refugee children in immigration court."

"That's wonderful," she said.

"Damn," Aiden muttered. "It was easier to hate you when I thought you were an ambulance chaser."

"At least I'm not a divorce attorney."

He pretended to be offended, but it would take more than my little jabs to crack his armor. "I don't only do divorces. Besides, what's wrong with divorce attorneys?"

I waved him off. "I'm sure you serve a purpose."

"Ever been divorced?"

"No."

"Then you don't know how useful we can be."

"Aiden was going to study corporate law," Aspen said. "Then his wife dumped him and he decided to be his own divorce attorney."

"A mistake, I'll admit." Aiden sighed. "Both the wife and not hiring a good lawyer."

He'd been married? Why did that make me jealous? We'd only been together one night. I had no claim on Aiden, but that envy crept through my veins like green sludge.

"Sorry." What was the polite way to comment on someone's divorce? I'd never been sure of the appropriate condolence. Or congratulation.

Aiden shrugged. "We got married in college. Both too young. I went in search of a divorce attorney and realized I couldn't afford one. My ex-wife, on the other hand, found a rather good lawyer and her team came out the victor."

"Probably because her parents paid for it." Aspen rolled her eyes. "I never liked her. She was too . . ." She looked to Aiden and signed something.

He laughed.

"What?" I asked.

"Don't tell her, Aiden." Aspen giggled. "It wasn't nice, and since we just met, I don't want you to think I'm crass. Let's just say his ex was prissy."

"Ah." I smiled, my imagination running wild with the actual term she'd used. Until today, I hadn't realized there were obscenities in sign language. It made sense. I just hadn't thought of it before.

"She was prissy. And evil. She stole my car," Aiden explained. "It was an old Mustang that I rebuilt in college. Once upon a time, I wanted to be an engineer. The reason

I couldn't afford an attorney was because I spent my extra cash on parts. Most of her extra money too. In the divorce, she asked for the car and won. Ten days after it was finalized, I saw it parked in my former yard with a *For Sale* sign in the windshield. Broke my damn heart to let go of that car."

Not the woman. Interesting. He was more upset about that car. "And you went from a newly divorced, wannabe engineer to a law student?"

"Pretty much. I finished undergrad at Montana State and decided to take the LSAT. I wanted to move as far away from Montana and my ex-wife as possible, so I found a law school in Texas. I graduated and worked at a firm there for a couple of years. Then I moved home to Prescott about six months ago."

The story was endearing. The entire lunch, really. Seeing Aiden's relationship with his sister and learning a bit about his past was softening me toward him. Almost enough that I'd forgotten how he'd tricked me. Almost.

Before that changed, it was time to go and put some distance between me and Aiden Archer.

I closed my laptop and stowed it away as the waitress arrived with their meals. I paid my check, then stood, pulled on my coat and smiled at Aspen. "It was lovely to meet you."

"You too."

"Aiden, it was . . ." I didn't bother finishing my sentence. I slung my tote over a shoulder and walked away.

"Lola?" he called.

I turned and arched my eyebrows. "Yes?"

"See you around."

"I doubt it."

"This is a small town."

I cocked my head. "Why does that sound like a threat?"

"A promise."

Damn this man for making me want to smile. "Doubtful."

But much to my chagrin, I wanted to see him again. Even if it was to argue and sling insults back and forth. Today's lunch had been . . . entertaining.

Aiden steepled his fingers in front of his chin. A challenge rested in his gaze.

Except there was no contest for him to win. I was leaving in four days. Until my departure, most of my time would be spent with Joann. She worked during the day, hence my solo working lunch. But our evenings would be spent together and she was taking Friday off so we could spend the day together.

Had Aiden already planned another negotiation session with Riley and Joann that I hadn't heard about yet? I'd advised her this morning to simply hand this over to her attorney and let him duke it out with Aiden. It was too painful for her to be in that room with Riley. Joann loved him despite it all. Riley loved her too.

But they were getting divorced.

And I would be returning home soon.

"Goodbye." I took two steps away, but then stopped and turned back. Yesterday, at Riley's, had been a low point. Part of me felt justified in punishing Aiden for his lies. The other part of me felt guilty for such a childish move. He did have really great teeth. They didn't deserve to suffer. "Oh, and, Aiden?"

"Yeah?"

"You might want to buy a new toothbrush."

His forehead furrowed. "What?"

I gave him my own wink. "Bye now."

―――――

"SERIOUSLY?" My jaw dropped as Aiden strolled into the coffee shop.

"Hello, Lola." He didn't go to the counter to order a beverage. No, he just plopped into the chair directly beside mine.

"Did you follow me here from the café?"

"Technically. Though technically, you're in my office. This is my favorite work spot when I'm in Calamity."

"Speaking of, why are you still in Calamity? Don't you have a dog to check on in Prescott? A litter box to empty? You've seen your sister. You've spent time with Riley. Don't you need to scurry home?"

"No dog. No cat. And it's been fun here this week. I forgot how much I loved Calamity. So there will be no *scurrying* for me today."

"You're not going to leave me alone, are you?"

He shook his head. "No. But . . ."

"I don't like people who say but and let it hang."

"But . . ."

I narrowed my eyes. "You really are infuriating."

"I know." He grinned. "Isn't it great?"

"Why are you here? Because you don't have a laptop, so don't pretend you're here to work."

"I have a proposition for you."

"Nope. No way. We did that on Saturday, remember?"

Aiden smiled and, damn it, my heart skipped. "Oh, I remember. And it was phenomenal. Don't deny it."

"I won't." Saturday night had been one of the most memorable in my life. Never before had sex been that incredible. And Aiden had made me feel lighter. After working seventy hours a week on grueling, heartrending cases, I needed levity. "But that doesn't mean I forgive you for lying to me."

"Would you forgive me if I apologized?"

"Is this another one of your tricks?"

"You aren't going to give an inch, are you?"

I shook my head. "Nope."

"Good. I like that about you." He smiled and, for the first time, it wasn't malicious or playful. It was genuine and proud. It reminded me a lot of the smiles he'd given me on Saturday night. "I didn't know who you were until Riley found Joann. I hung back to give them some space. And by that point, I was under your spell. I should have told you who I was, but you were too beautiful. I didn't want to walk away."

"Oh." The air rushed from my lungs. As far as apologies went, that was, well . . . perfect.

"Saturday night wasn't a trick. I wanted you. Badly. I thought that maybe you were playing me, but I didn't care. There was no gain in it for me."

"No gain?"

"Legally." He laughed. "No legal gain. Obviously, I got something that night."

"Me. You got me."

He reached for a stray lock of hair by my ear, ready to tuck it behind my ear, but stopped himself before his fingers touched the strand. Instead, he dragged a hand through his own hair. "Truce?"

"How do you know I'm not playing you?"

He barked a laugh so loud it drew attention from the nearby tables. "Nah. You were too mad yesterday. I don't think you're that good of an actress."

"Yesterday you suspected I crashed into you on purpose. That I was trying to get information for the mediation."

"Changed my mind. The more I'm around you, the more I can tell I'm genuinely under your skin."

I crossed my arms over my chest. "And you think we can just call a truce?"

He nodded. "Yup."

It would have been easier to hold a grudge if I didn't believe him. "Fine."

"Excellent. Now back to my proposition." He picked up my coffee cup and took a drink.

"Hey!"

He waved it off. "You deserve that after whatever it is you did to my toothbrush."

"Fair enough."

"Back to my proposition."

"I'm on pins and needles here," I said dryly, tapping my fingers on the table.

"Joann and Riley."

"Oh no." I held up my hands before he could continue. "I'm not getting involved. I was moral support only during the mediation."

"You really want to help your friend?"

"Of course."

"Good. Because we're going to get them back together."

# CHAPTER FOUR

AIDEN ARCHER WAS A ROMANTIC.

I hadn't expected that.

After he'd explained his plan at the coffee shop yesterday, I'd been hopeless to resist. Joann and Riley loved each other. They might be awful at communicating, but they'd learn after a decade of marriage. Hopefully.

"This is a nice theater." I looked around the lobby, pretending to take it all in when really, I was searching for Aiden.

We'd exchanged phone numbers. Then while Joann had been at work, we'd met earlier today to hash out Operation Reconciliation.

It was basic. Get Joann and Riley in the same place and hope that they'd talk, not fight. I had three days left in Calamity and we were going to use all three if necessary.

Tonight, we'd be at the theater. It wasn't a large place. The lobby was just big enough for a ticket office, a small concession stand and shuffling room between the two theaters.

"It's cute, right?" Joann smiled.

"Super cute." Oh my lovely Joann. Totally oblivious that I was shamelessly betraying her.

It was for her own good.

"Good idea on the movie," she said. "I haven't been here in ages."

"You and Riley didn't go on movie dates?"

"No." She frowned at the mention of his name. "Not since we got Clarence. He didn't want to leave the puppy home alone."

Poor, sweet, innocent Clarence was the reason his family was breaking up. Riley showered his dog with affection when he should have also spread that attention to his wife.

And Joann had gotten jealous. It was something she'd never admit, especially because she'd bought the dog. She was too stubborn to tell Riley to stop spoiling the dog and remember he was married.

"Should we find seats?" she asked.

There was no sign of Aiden and Riley, which meant they were in the theater. *Perfect.* "Um . . . what about snacks?"

"Rock, paper, scissors for who has to wait in line."

"Okay." I hid a smile. She was making this too easy.

In college, Joann and I always used to play rock, paper, scissors for who had to get the snacks. Her habits hadn't changed. She'd go for rock first.

"One. Two. Three. Shoot," I said, smiling at her predictability. "Paper covers rock."

"Damn," she muttered. "Okay, what do you want?"

"Popcorn. Diet Coke. Should we split some candy?"

"Sure. What kind?"

"Surprise me." I took her coat from her arm and made my way into the theater, scanning each row as I walked.

And there they were.

Just like we'd planned, Aiden was sitting in the middle of the room with Riley by his side. Also according to plan, I took the chairs directly behind theirs. If those had been full, I would have sat in front of them.

The lights were dim and the previews started as I settled into the chair. Aiden didn't glance back or say a word, but there was an awareness there. He sat a little straighter. He cleared his throat, like he could feel my aura in the room and the electricity between us.

The third preview was playing when Joann shuffled down the row, crouching so as not to block the screen from the people behind us. The theater wasn't packed, but it was busy enough that it would keep Joann and Riley from a screaming match.

Joann had returned Clarence to Riley's on Sunday, but she'd made sure he wasn't there when she put the dog back in his kennel. Other than texts, they hadn't spoken since the shouting match during mediation.

The goal tonight wasn't to let Riley and Joann talk. No, no. Talking was bad. Tonight's plan was exactly the opposite. We wanted them to see one another. To know that they were within touching distance. And that they had no choice but to sit there and suffer through it.

A movie was the perfect opportunity because they couldn't throw punches.

Joann smiled, still clueless to her surroundings, and plopped into her seat. She handed me my pop and gave me the bucket of popcorn. "These are great sea—what the hell?"

She'd spotted the back of Riley's head.

"What?" I feigned innocence.

"What?" she hissed, pointing a finger at her husband. "How did you not notice them?"

"Who?"

She pointed again, her eyes bulging.

"Oh." I winced. "Sorry. I was looking at my phone."

Her expression flattened. "You're killing me."

"Do you mind?" Aiden turned. "We're trying to watch a movie."

"You." I picked up a piece of popcorn from the bucket and threw it at his head. Not part of the act but fun nonetheless.

"Me." He popped the kernel in his mouth and grinned as he chewed.

Riley turned, and for the briefest second, his face lit up with joy. Then it fell. "Hey."

"Hi," she murmured.

"Maybe we should go," I suggested, then held my breath. *Say no. Say no. Say no.*

"No," Joann said. God, I loved my stubborn friend. There was no way she'd let Riley chase her out of the theater. "We already paid a fortune and I want to see this. If they are uncomfortable, they can leave."

Riley moved to stand but Aiden tossed his arm on the back of the seats and crossed one ankle over a knee. "I'm not uncomfortable. How about you, Riley?"

One question and he'd painted Riley into a corner.

"Not at all." Riley resumed his seat, cast one last glance at Joann, then faced the screen.

For two hours, he sat stiff as a board. Joann used her nervous energy to devour the entire bucket of popcorn and a box of peanut M&M's while I struggled to keep my focus on the show.

My gaze kept wandering toward Aiden's disheveled hair. It might look a mess, but it was so silky soft, I had to sit on my hands so I wouldn't be tempted to touch. It was impossible to concentrate on anything with him so close.

Aiden was the only one who seemed unaffected by our proximity. Not once did he turn to look. Not once did he shift or fidget. He enjoyed the movie, and when it was over, he stood and gave me that blinding smile. "Good movie."

My mouth went dry as he stretched his arms above his head. The T-shirt he was wearing rode up his ribs, showing a hint of the washboard abs underneath. The waistband of his jeans sat low on the V of his hips.

Aiden bent to pick up the coat that had fallen to the floor, and in that one move, he had me drooling. The muscled, sculpted ass that had gotten me into this mess in the first place was right there for my viewing pleasure.

"Come on, Lola."

I blinked, tearing my eyes away from Aiden's delicious backside.

Joann had her hands on her hips, her coat on and the trash from the snack haul ready for the garbage can.

"Sorry." Springing into action, I hurried to collect my coat and purse, then followed her as she rushed down the aisle.

She didn't spare Riley one look. Not one. She'd endured the movie, but that was the limit.

*Damn.*

Was this going to work? Yes, they'd spent two hours in the same room, but we hadn't accomplished anything.

Before Joann could rush us out the door, I took one last glance over my shoulder at Aiden. Like he knew the fears swirling in my head, he gave me a reassuring nod.

*I hope you know what you're doing, Archer.*

———

"THIS ISN'T WORKING," I whisper-yelled.

"Hell." Aiden dragged a hand through his hair, making the ends stick up at all angles. "Those two are so damn stubborn."

We'd gone from Joann screaming at Riley in the mediation room to a tense and awkward movie where she'd glared daggers into his neck. Now it was silence over dinner. Complete and utter silence. She wasn't even speaking to me.

It was so bad that I'd finally escaped our table and the booming scrape of her fork and knife to *use the bathroom.* Aiden, not one to let the sign for the women's room stop him, had snuck in after me. Thankfully, there were no other ladies in the stalls.

"Maybe we should have picked a different restaurant," Aiden said.

With only two nights left, Joann and I had decided to come to the fanciest restaurant in Calamity. It was supposed to be a celebration, not only for my visit, but for her impending divorce.

Really, it had been my suggestion because Aiden was dragging Riley here too.

The moment they'd walked through the door, Joann had gone silent.

Riley, on the other hand, had decided to play this the opposite way. He laughed. He talked with other patrons. He joked with Aiden at their table two away from ours. Riley was making such a show of having a good time, it was clear the man was miserable.

And every time his voice carried across the room and hit Joann's ears, she sank a little deeper into herself.

Torture was not what I wanted for my friend.

"We're going to go," I said. "I can't make her sit and endure this. She's miserable."

"So is Riley." Aiden closed his eyes and blew out a deep breath. "He's pretending."

"Maybe we should call off tomorrow night."

We were supposed to be dragging our friends to Jane's, the local bar. After two consecutive days seeing one another, Aiden and I had hoped that they'd strike up a conversation. That they'd realize how much they missed each other.

And after a few drinks, they'd shed their inhibitions and dive straight into makeup sex.

It was a dream. A silly dream. Joann and Riley were worlds apart. Maybe they'd already accepted what Aiden and I hadn't yet.

They were over.

Our scheming was only hurting them both.

"That didn't go like I'd expected," I said.

"Me neither." Aiden sighed. "I'm not a quitter but . . ."

"There's that hanging but again."

He grinned. "Had to sneak one more in."

Silence hung in the restroom, awkward and long. I took in the trash can overflowing with paper towels. The water drops drying beside the two sinks. Why couldn't I just say goodbye and go? Why did it feel like I'd miss something when I left here?

"Well, we tried," I said, prolonging the inevitable.

"I, uh . . ." He rubbed the back of his neck.

"Thanks for try—"

The door opened and a woman came inside. Her jaw dropped when she spotted Aiden. "Oh, uh . . ." She checked the door to see if she had the correct bathroom.

"Sorry. I'm maintenance." Aiden gave her a smile as the lie dripped off his tongue. "The toilet is broken, and you do not want to come in here." He scrunched up his nose as he ushered her out. Then as soon as she was clear, he slammed the door and twisted the lock. "Where were we?"

"I was leaving. It's time to put an end to this awful idea."

"Awful?" His jaw clenched. "It wasn't awful. And you were just as much a part of it as I was."

"I went along with it, but this was *your* idea. You approached me, remember? I should have known it wouldn't work with Joann. She's too stubborn. And you should have known that Riley—"

My stomach dropped. Wait. Had I just fallen into another one of this man's traps? Had he played me again?

"Riley, what?" Aiden asked.

"You knew they wouldn't get back together, didn't you?"

"Huh?"

"Was this another one of your tricks? Maybe you thought you'd soften Joann up, and then when it came time to return to the mediation room, she'd be more willing to give in to Riley." Oh. My. God. How had I not thought of this? "It was, wasn't it? This was always about winning the divorce. About getting Clarence."

"What are you talking about?"

I gaped at him. "I can't believe you. Is winning really that important? She's a person. She's a beautiful, wonderful person with a broken heart because your client" —I shoved my finger in his chest—"is a cheating asshole."

"Riley didn't cheat."

"Emotionally, he cheated. He betrayed her trust."

Aiden's jaw dropped. "Are you fucking serious?"

Oh, yes. I was serious. My eyes narrowed. "Stay away from me. Stay away from Joann."

Aiden shook his head, dumbfounded. "You really think I'd hurt Joann so Riley would get the dog in the divorce?"

"Yes." Maybe.

He winced. A flash of pain crossed his face and I knew I'd read it all wrong. In the course of thirty seconds, I'd twisted his actions in my head and acted like a jerk. What was wrong with me? Had I really become this cynical? I saw a lot of bad people with my job, people who hurt kids. But that didn't mean every adult was a monster. Certainly not the man standing in front of me.

"Aiden, I'm—"

He didn't give me the time to apologize. He flipped the door's lock and was gone in an instant.

When I returned to the dining room, his table was empty.

———

"I NEED A MARGARITA."

I was off the couch before Joann finished her sentence. "Brilliant idea."

She laughed, standing too. "Then off to Jane's we go."

*Jane's.* I opened my mouth to stop her but swallowed my words. Calamity Jane's was the bar where Aiden and I had planned to stage our third run-in with Joann and Riley. The last thing I wanted before I left in the morning was to admit to my friend that Aiden and I had been plotting against her.

But he wouldn't still be bringing Riley, right? I doubted Aiden wanted to set eyes on me ever again after my restroom accusations last night.

So when she hauled me out the door, I didn't protest. *Jane's it is.*

Fifteen minutes later, after we'd decided primping was unnecessary, we were at a table with two fresh margaritas. The bar had a three-to-one ratio of men to women, and a ten-to-one ratio of beer signs to men. It was dark and had the faint smell of smoke. The bartender, who Joann had informed me was also the owner, looked like she would have been comfortable living in the days when cowboys tied their horses to hitching posts out front and settled disagreements with pistols instead of lawyers.

There was really nothing quite like a small-town Montana bar.

"Cheers." I raised my glass. "To your newly single status."

"Cheers." She clinked her glass to mine and we each took a long sip. "I wish you weren't leaving. It feels like you just got here."

"I know." The week had gone too fast.

Joann had needed to work all week, and though I'd done my best to clear my calendar, I'd spent my time keeping up on emails and taking the occasional call. I was behind on a case, and when I returned home, I'd have to scramble to catch up. Unfortunately, with my coffee-shop rendezvous with Aiden to play matchmakers, the week had proved to be full of distractions.

Namely, one handsome distraction.

A man I doubted I'd ever see again.

"Next time, maybe you can come visit me for a week," I said.

"I'd like that. It's been a while since I was in Port— nooooooo. Not again," she moaned, her gaze traveling past my shoulder to the door.

"What?" I twisted and my heart stopped.

Aiden was smiling as he walked in the door. Behind him, Riley was laughing. The two of them strolled into the bar, shrugging their jackets and stomping their boots as they scanned the room.

Riley's laughter died and both men paled when they spotted us at a table.

"Why?" Joann whispered. "Why can't I avoid him?"

I turned to the table and gave her a sad smile. "Small

town. Of course you'll run into the person you don't want to see. But it's more than that. I, um . . . have a confession. Better take a drink."

She obeyed as I explained to her that Aiden and I had hatched a plan to try and force a reconciliation. The hurt on her face made me feel like Clarence's poo.

"Why would you do that?" she asked.

"Because I love you." I reached across the table and covered her hand with mine. "And because you love Riley and Riley loves you. This is crazy, Joann. You are punishing him. And yourself. That man loves you so much. There's no way he had an emotional affair. You're the only woman he can see."

"He told *that woman* about us. About me. Do you have any idea how humiliating it is that the entire town knows I can't get pregnant?"

"Riley shouldn't have done it. You're right to be angry. But I suspect it was because he was feeling just as lost as you are."

For a brief moment, I thought my words sank in. Then her gaze hardened, and she plucked her keys off the table and shot out of her chair.

"Joann." I tried to stop her but she was already marching for the door. "Damn it."

Hurrying to collect my purse and coat, I stood in a flourish, dropping some cash on the table to pay our tab. When I turned, ready to sprint after my best friend, I ran into a wall.

"Oof."

"Sorry." Aiden's hands came to my biceps, steadying

me. Then he let me go like his hands were burning and took one step away.

"I have to go. I have to catch Joann."

"Riley ran after her."

I looked past him just in time to see the door close and the place where Riley had been standing empty. "Oh."

"I told him about . . . you know. He was pissed. Told me I owed him a few drinks at the bar. I didn't think you'd come."

"I didn't think you'd be here either. I just told Joann why she can't seem to avoid Riley. She's not really happy with me."

"I can see that." He backed away another step. "Take care."

"Aiden." I stretched for him, brushing his arm to get him to stop. "About what I said in the restroom yesterday, I'm sorry."

"You don't think much of me, do you?"

"No, on the contrary. For a man I don't know very well, I'm afraid to admit that maybe I think too much. The truth is, I went looking for a reason not to trust you so that when I leave here, I can forget about you. Only, I don't know if I'll ever forget about you."

The words were out of my mouth before I could consider the ramifications. My cards were on the table, but there was no hiding it.

I liked Aiden. I liked him a lot.

And that scared the hell out of me.

"I'd better get going and check on Joann," I said as he stood there, unspeaking. "If she didn't leave me here already. It's a long walk in the cold to her house. Does Calamity have Uber?"

He shook his head.

"Thanks." I steeled my spine and held out my hand. "It was nice to meet you, Aiden Archer."

His grip enveloped mine, but it was his gaze that held me captive. "Same to you, Lola Jennings."

*Aiden Archer.*

An unexpected surprise. A man I wouldn't forget for a long, long time.

I stepped closer, going on my tiptoes to press a kiss to his cheek. "Goodbye."

"Bye."

My heart was in my throat with every step toward the door. This was for the best. It was time to get back to Portland and resume my normal life.

So I didn't look back.

Until he called my name.

"Lola, wait."

# CHAPTER FIVE

"YES," I breathed. Aiden hadn't asked me a question, but whatever he wanted, the answer was yes.

He stepped closer and the rest of the bar faded into shadows. "When are you leaving?"

"Tomorrow." Joann would drive me the two hours to Bozeman, then I'd hop on a plane and be back to Portland before dinner.

"Then I want tonight." His hands slipped into tendrils of my hair as he leaned down, brushing his lips against mine. "What do you say?"

"I say, yes." A smile tugged at my mouth as he brushed another kiss to my lower lip. I closed my eyes, ready for him to devour me whole, but suddenly the heat from his chest was gone and I was spinning.

Aiden gripped my hand and towed me out of the bar, his long strides making me jog to keep up.

I scanned the sidewalks, searching for Joann, but she

was nowhere to be seen. Her car was still where we'd parked it though. Maybe she'd walked around the block.

"I'm a horrible friend," I said as Aiden rushed me to his truck. The right thing to do would be to go to her house and beg for forgiveness. But Aiden . . . this was the last night. Deep in my soul, I knew that if I didn't take this chance for one last night together, I'd regret it for the rest of my days.

"Send her a text. She'll be fine." He unlocked the doors and flung the passenger seat open.

I hopped inside, taking his face in my hands before he could escape. I was about to steal the kiss I'd wanted in the bar, but he shook his head and ripped himself free.

"If I kiss you now, we'll never make it to bed. And I really want you in bed."

I giggled. "Okay."

Aiden's hazel eyes were locked on mine, the darkened lust swirling in their brilliant colors as he gave me that wicked smile. "I've got a surprise for you."

"I hate surprises."

"Why does that not shock me?" He slammed my door, jogging to the driver's side and wasting no time getting us on the road.

"What about Riley?" Aiden had ditched him as quickly as I'd ditched Joann.

"He's a big boy. He knows how to get home."

"Don't you think it will be awkward if he comes home later and hears us having sex?"

My question earned me a shrug.

"Aiden," I warned.

"Shh. Trust me."

I did trust him. After less than a week together, I trusted him, despite my accusations in the restroom. Maybe because he was a good friend to Riley and brother to Aspen. Maybe because he'd been honest with me. Maybe because there was something happening between us that felt . . . significant.

So I sat quietly, my knees bouncing in anticipation, as he drove us through Calamity.

"This is not Riley's," I whispered when he pulled into an unfamiliar driveway. The single-story home was small but charming and quaint. The light in the window cast a soft glow on the snow-covered yard.

"It's a vacation rental. I moved in here yesterday morning. Before the restaurant."

"Why?"

He pulled into the driveway and parked. Then he leaned forward, one wrist dangling over the steering wheel as he twisted to face me. "Guess."

"Because of me."

"I hoped maybe we could have another night before you left. And I thought you'd be more comfortable here."

My heart skipped. "Thank you."

"Come on." He jerked his chin and we both climbed out of the truck. He met me on the sidewalk, taking my hand and leading me to the door. When he opened it for me, the scent of cinnamon potpourri and Aiden's own cedar spice filled my nose.

He didn't give me time to look around the house. He kicked the door closed and then he was everywhere. His lips consumed my own. His tongue twined with mine. His hands roamed, appreciating every curve as he stripped me of my coat and worked the button free on my jeans.

"Bed," I panted, tearing at his jacket.

He shrugged it off, shuffling us down a hallway as we left a trail of clothing in our wake.

My hands traced the hard plane of his chest. My lips molded to his pebbled rosy nipples. My heart thundered when he laid me down and made love to me all night long.

Aiden worshiped my body. He made me feel alive and cherished. He ignited a passion in my soul I'd only felt one time before. Saturday, with him.

And when I finally drifted off to sleep, it was in his arms.

Wishing, for the first time in my life, the sun wouldn't rise.

---

"WHAT TIME'S YOUR FLIGHT?" Aiden asked as he drove me to Joann's. He had one hand on the wheel. The other clutched mine so tightly my knuckles were squished together.

Or maybe I was the one clinging to him.

Last night had been one of the best in my life. This week had been something special, even with the scheming, the banter and the battle of wits. Maybe that was why it had been so special. Aiden had a way of stripping away my starch and poise. He kept me on my toes. Nothing he did was predictable.

He was unlike any man I'd ever met, and I wasn't ready to say goodbye.

"Twelve forty-five."

"Text me when you get home?" he asked.

"Sure."

We both knew I wasn't going to text.

There was no future here. My life was in Portland. His was in Prescott, a town I hadn't even seen. This was simply a vacation hookup. A Valentine's Day that had lasted a week.

Aiden was a fling. A memorable fling, but a fling nonetheless.

We'd had two all-night sex marathons. Two nights. That was it. Aiden didn't want a long-distance relationship and neither did I, not really. I didn't want to survive months and months of texts and phone calls and the occasional visit only to have my heart broken in the end.

After only a week, the weight of our farewell was so heavy that I wanted to curl into a ball and cry. How would it be after months? A year? No, it was time to go home. I'd save the crying for when I got home to my quiet and lonely apartment.

"This was . . ."

God, what was the word? Fun sounded so cheap. Amazing sounded trivial.

Life altering. That was the term, but admitting that would make this all the more painful.

"Yeah." Aiden nodded, giving me a sad smile. "Yeah, it was."

Did he feel this too? Last night, when he'd been on top of me, moving inside me, his eyes had been so full of longing and hope.

This wasn't love. It was too soon to call this love.

If only we lived in the same state.

Aiden pulled up to Joann's much too soon and the ache in my chest spiked.

Why did this hurt so much? Neither of us let go of our linked hands as he parked. He clutched me. I held on tight, turning to take in his handsome face one last time.

I'd miss those beautiful hazel eyes. I'd miss his mischievous smile. When he flashed that grin my way, it was hard not to smile myself.

I didn't smile often enough. Until Aiden, I hadn't realized how few smiles were in my life.

Until Aiden, I hadn't had a lot of reasons to smile.

I stretched my free arm across the cab, running my fingers through the mess of his dark hair. "Take care of yourself."

He lifted his hand to trace my chin, holding it as he leaned closer for a kiss.

One last kiss.

I tore my hand free of his so I could frame his face and pull him closer. With my eyes squeezed so tightly that the tears couldn't fall, I kissed him with everything I had to give. And when the lump in my throat burned like a hot coal, I tore myself away and hurried from the truck, not looking back as I crossed Joann's freshly shoveled sidewalk.

I slipped inside the house, pressing my back to the door, and waited for the rumble of Aiden's engine to disappear down the street.

"Ouch," I whispered, pressing a hand to my heart when the noise disappeared. A few tears worked free and I swiped them away.

"Hey!" Joann rushed into the living room, cinching a robe around her waist.

I shoved off the door and forced a smile, sniffing away the tears. "Hi. I'm really sorry about last night."

She waved it off. "It's okay. Your heart was in the right place."

I narrowed my gaze. Joann was a beautiful, loving person, but forgiveness was not her most shining trait. Riley and her divorce were a prime example. So why was she so quick to forgive me for playing her this week?

Something wasn't right.

I glanced around the room, then took in the flush of her face. Just as I was working it out in my head, a click of nails echoed on the hardwood floors.

Clarence emerged from the hallway, his tail wagging wildly.

My jaw dropped. "Riley's here, isn't he?"

"Uh . . . hey, Lola." Riley peeked out from behind the corner of the kitchen. His T-shirt was rumpled, probably from being on the floor all night long.

"What does this mean?" I asked Joann as hope swelled. A saved marriage would go a long way toward improving my morning.

"We're not getting divorced," Riley answered, striding across the room to Joann's side.

"No, we're not." Joann stood on her toes and pressed a kiss to his jaw. "He infuriates me, but I love him."

"Love you too, babe."

"How? When?"

"Last night." Joann shrugged. "I was mad at you, so I didn't have the energy to be mad at him. When he followed me out of the bar, we sat in my car and talked for hours in the dark. I don't want him to go to the movies without me. I don't want to eat a nice dinner at a restaurant when he's not at my table. I don't want to live in separate homes and have different last names."

"I'm so happy for you guys."

"I'm happy for us too." Joann dabbed at the corner of her eye. "Even if it's only the two of us and Clarence, we'll be happy."

He kissed her forehead. "It'll happen when the time is right."

"I hope so," she whispered.

"What do you say, boy?" Riley crouched down to rub behind Clarence's ears. "Want to have a sibling one day?"

Joann had hearts in her eyes as she watched Clarence lick Riley's face.

I was returning to Portland today a little sad, a lot lonely. But to see Joann and Riley together again, it was worth it. Maybe it wasn't meeting a great guy that had made this trip such a turning point.

Maybe this trip had shown me that my work-centered life needed to change.

Until this week, a Valentine's Day alone would have sounded like bliss. Now I was twisted in a knot and I didn't quite want to untangle the threads.

It was time to live. To be the one who entered a booty-shaking contest just to see if I could win.

It was time to live more like Aiden.

"Okay." Joann sighed, dragging her eyes away from her husband. "We'd better get going to the airport."

"I'll go pack." I forced a smile, making my way through the living room.

"Where were you last night?" Joann asked before I could disappear.

I glanced back and shrugged. "With Aiden."

"Are you two—"

"No. We were just having fun. I'll be ready soon."

"Okay." Joann gave me a sad smile as she leaned her cheek into Riley's chest.

An hour later, she was driving me along the streets of Calamity, headed for the highway. And two hours after that, we were hugging on the airport sidewalk.

"I'm going to miss you."

I squeezed her tighter. "You too. I'm happy for you and Riley."

"I owe you."

"No, you don't." They would have worked it out eventually. Hopefully.

"Call me when you get home."

"I will." I let her go and collected my luggage, then with a wave, I rolled it inside and toward security.

Every step felt heavy. Joann must have snuck bricks into my suitcase because with each step, it tugged me backward.

"Come on," I muttered, heaving it faster. Too fast. The wheels skidded forward and one of them rammed into my heel. "Damn it."

Stupid ballet flats. These were going in the garbage as soon as—

"Maybe you should let me take the suitcase."

My head whipped up from my feet.

"Aiden?" I blinked to make sure he was real. "What are you doing here?"

He let go of the handle on his own suitcase and unzipped his coat, pulling out his phone. He woke it up and turned the screen my way.

"You bought a plane ticket?" I squinted, leaning closer to make sure I wasn't hallucinating. But there it was, in clear letters. He was flying to Portland. Today. On my flight. "Why?"

"I have this theory." He returned the phone to his pocket and stepped so close that I had to tip my head back to keep his gaze.

"What's your theory?"

His fingertips drifted into my hair, toying with the ends. "When you meet someone who scares you, that's probably a person you want to keep in your life."

"Like a serial killer? Because I'm going to have to disagree with your theory."

Aiden chuckled. "Different kind of scared. The good kind of scared."

"There's a good kind of scared?"

"Sure." He shrugged. "Before you graduate. Before you have kids. Before you buy a house."

"Before you hop onstage and shake your ass in front of an entire town."

"That was not scary. I was guaranteed to win."

I rolled my eyes. "You are the most arrogant man."

"Please. You've seen my ass. I've still got fingernail marks on it from last night. That's not arrogance. That's just me stating facts, baby."

My face flushed. "Oops. Maybe I did get a little carried away with the nails last night."

"Will you shut up so I can make my point?" he asked.

I pulled my lips between my teeth.

"Lola, you scare me. From the very first night, you scared the hell out of me."

My breath hitched. "You scare me too."

"So I've decided I'd better keep you in my life. What do you have to say about that?"

"Long distance is hard," I said.

"Yeah, it is. But I'm hoping we can stick it out for a while. If this thing goes the way I think it's going to go, we'll make the tough decisions later."

My heart hammered in my chest. "You're serious? This is really happening?"

His arms banded around my back. "I'm serious."

"This was not how I thought this day was going to go." The smile on my face stretched so wide it hurt as I slid my hands around his hips, burying them in the back pockets of his Wranglers.

I really, really loved Wranglers.

"I like to keep things interesting."

"Why does that sound like a threat?"

He bent, laughing as he dropped a kiss to the corner of my mouth. "A promise."

EPILOGUE

ONE YEAR LATER . . .

"What is that smell?" I twisted in my seat, searching and sniffing. The smell was coming from the direction of the buffet table, but it didn't belong to any of the items I'd preapproved for the caterer. No, this smelled . . . fried.

We were not having fried food at our wedding.

"Aiden?"

A slow grin stretched across my husband's face.

"What did you do?"

He shrugged.

I pointed my finger at his nose. "Answer the question, Aiden Archer."

"It's nothing, Lola Archer."

If he thought using my new last name was going to soften me up, he was . . . right. Damn it, he was right. "You know how I feel about surprises."

"I have a theory about that."

Joann groaned beside me. "Not another theory."

70

"Imagine living with him," I muttered. "You miss half the theories because you're in Calamity."

Six months ago, I'd packed up my Portland apartment and moved into Aiden's house in Prescott. It had been an adjustment to small-town life. There was no such thing as twenty-four-hour grocery delivery or Uber Eats. Working remotely for my firm in Portland had its challenges. But I got to fall asleep in Aiden's arms every night and wake up to his smile in the morning.

I was winning at life.

Plus, having my best friend two hours away was a perk. Especially now that she and Riley were pregnant with a baby girl due this summer.

"What's the theory?" Riley asked Aiden as he toyed with the strap on Joann's bridesmaid dress.

Both men were dressed in charcoal suits while Joann wore black. I was in a white lace wedding gown. The red roses on the reception tables were the only nod to Valentine's Day tomorrow.

Our wedding date was exactly one year after I'd met Aiden at the Testicle Festival.

We were skipping the festivities in Calamity this year. Instead, we'd thrown a party of our own in Prescott. Fifty of our closest family members and friends were here to celebrate our wedding day.

"My theory is that Lola actually likes surprises," Aiden said.

"Your theory is bunk."

"You always complain about them, but . . ."

I blinked, waiting for him to finish.

He just grinned.

That smell hit my nose again. "What did you do, Aiden?"

He handed me my glass of champagne, probably to soothe my nerves. Maybe he thought I wouldn't throw it in his face because it was our wedding. He was right. But nothing would save him from my wrath tomorrow. "It's nothing."

"Tell me."

"I had the caterers add a last-minute addition to the menu since we aren't going to Testy Fest tonight."

My jaw dropped.

"You didn't." Joann burst into a fit of giggles.

"Rocky Mountain oysters?" Riley asked.

"Yep." The Cheshire cat grin on Aiden's face was infuriating. And endearing.

I wanted to argue, throw his theory in his face, but I always ended up enjoying his surprises. At least all the surprises before this one. "I'm not eating one."

"You don't have to."

"Are there any other surprises I should know about?"

"When we get home, I'm going to pull on my Wranglers and dance around for you." He leaned forward and took my earlobe between his teeth.

"Now you're talking." A shiver rolled down my spine. "Anything else?"

"Maybe."

"Are you going to tell me?"

"No."

"You're impossible."

He chuckled and leaned away. The look of devotion in those hazel eyes made me melt, the grease stink and menu addition forgiven. If he wanted to surprise me, I'd tease him but never make him stop.

"What did I promise you?" he asked.

"To keep things interesting."

"And?"

"And I love you."

He dropped his forehead to mine. "I love you too."

# ABOUT THE AUTHOR

Devney Perry is a *Wall Street Journal* and *USA Today* bestselling author of over forty romance novels. After working in the technology industry for a decade, she abandoned conference calls and project schedules to pursue her passion for writing. She was born and raised in Montana and now lives in Washington with her husband and two sons.

Don't miss out on the latest book news.
Subscribe to her newsletter!
www.devneyperry.com